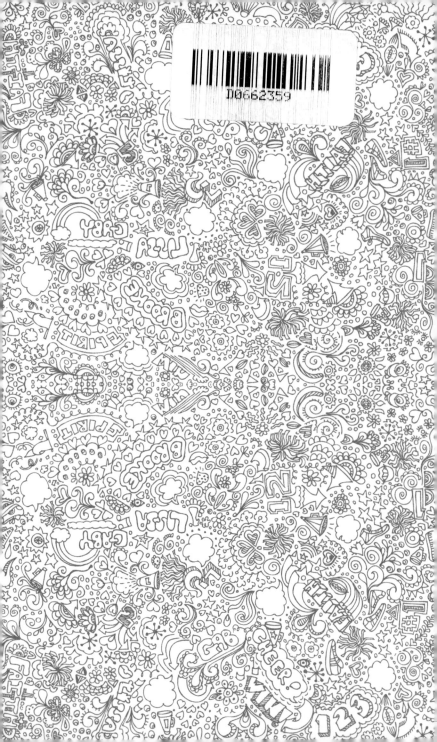

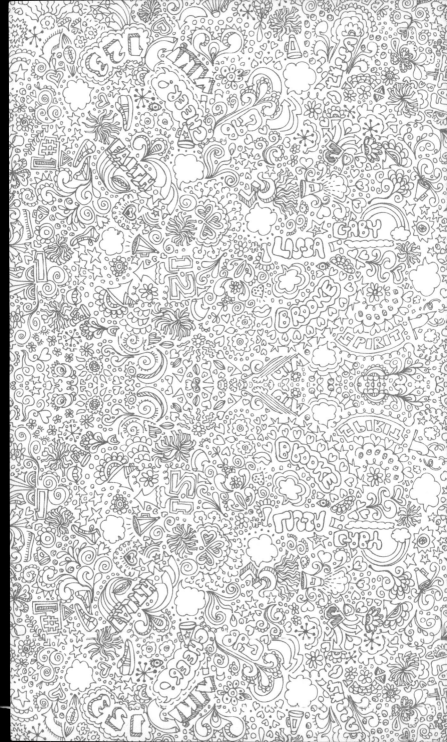

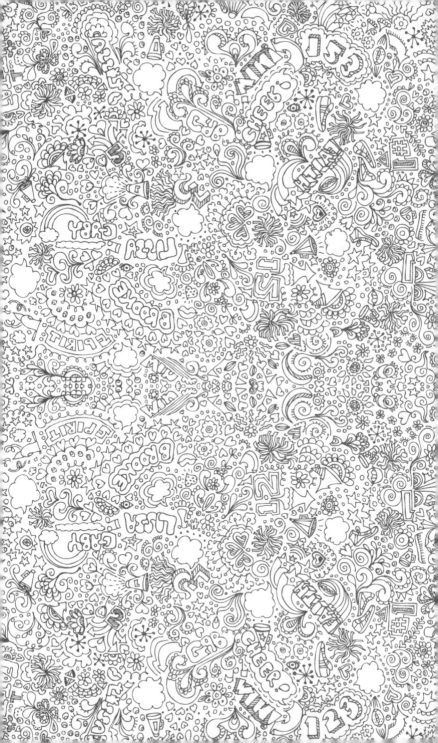

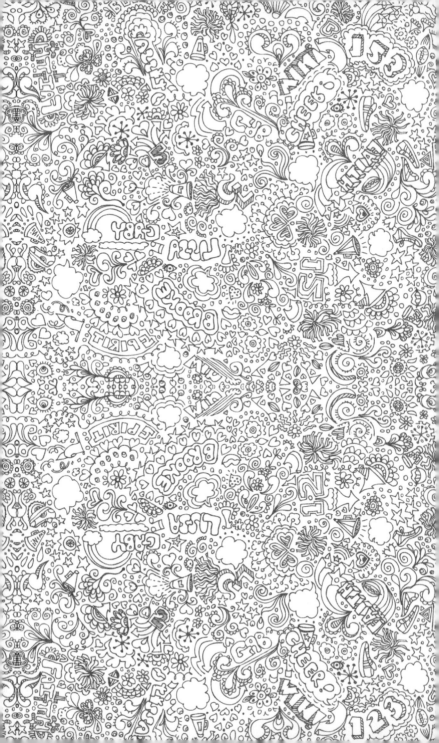

Team Cheer

Brooke's
QUEST
FOR
CAPTAIN

Team Cheer is published by Stone Arch Books
A Capstone Imprint
1710 Roe Crest Drive
North Mankato, Minnesota 56003
www.capstonepub.com

Library of Congress Cataloging-in-Publication Data
Jones, Jen.
  Brooke's quest for captain / by Jen Jones.
    p. cm. — (Team Cheer)
  Summary: Brooke Perrino really wants to be captain of her school cheerleading team, but she is having trouble with eighth-grade algebra and suddenly she is beginning to doubt her ability to handle the pressure.
  ISBN-13: 978-1-4342-4250-1 (paperback)
  1. Cheerleading—Juvenile fiction. 2. Middle schools—Juvenile fiction.
3. Friendship—Juvenile fiction. 4. Self-confidence—Juvenile fiction.
5. Competition (Psychology)—Juvenile fiction. [1. Cheerleading—Fiction.
2. Middle schools—Fiction. 3. Schools—Fiction. 4. Friendship—Fiction.
5. Self-confidence—Fiction. 6. Competition (Psychology)—Fiction.] I. Title.
  PZ7.J720311Br 2011
  813.54—dc22   2011001998

Cover Illustrations: Liz Adams
Artistic Elements: Shutterstock: belle,
blue67design, Nebojsa I, notkoo
Cheer Pattern: Sandy D'Antonio

Printed in the United State of America in Stevens Point, Wisconsin.
022014   008034

Brooke's QUEST FOR CAPTAIN

by Jen Jones

capstone

Greenview Middle School Cheer Team Roster

NAME	CLASS
Britt Bolton	7th
Kate Ellis	7th
Gaby Fuller	8th
Sheena Hays	8th
Faith Higgins	8th
Ella Jenkins	8th

Friend, fashionista, and all-around fabulous, Gaby gets us all going with her perkiness.

Faith may be a newbie to cheerleading, but not to being a great friend. What a sweetheart!

Not to be mean, but Ella is sort of a nightmare!

Lissa is one tough cookie! She protects all of her friends, and I'm glad to have her in my corner.

This is me! future captain? I hope so!

Kacey Kosir	8th
Melissa "Lissa" Marks	8th
Trina Mathews	8th
Brooke Perrino	8th
Mackenzie Potz	7th
Maddie Todd	7th

Coach: Bernadette Adkins

I think Mackenzie is my main competition for captain.

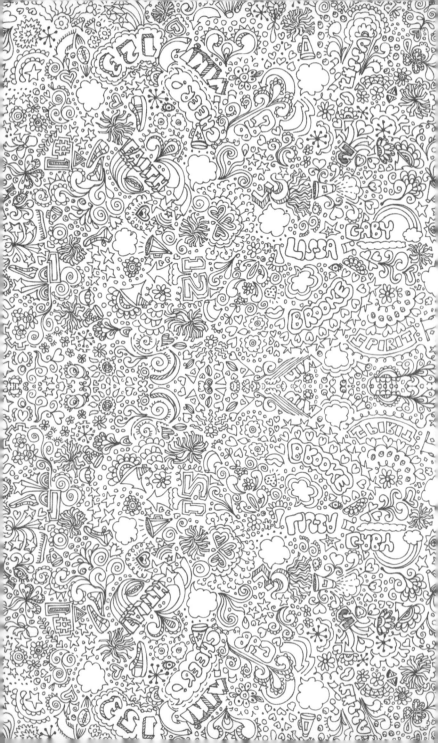

Chapter 1

"A cheerleader without poms is like peanut butter without jelly. Dolce without Gabbana. A pen . . . without ink!" said Gaby Fuller, dramatically clutching a shiny pom to her chest.

Giggling, I playfully swatted the always-silly Gaby with my own pom. "Well, you better start fluffing, or none of us will have poms to use this season," I said.

Reluctantly, Gaby sat back down to rejoin the rest of us. "I thought cheerleading was supposed to be glamorous," she grumbled. Diva-like as she could be, she had a point. Cheerleading definitely had tons of fun perks, but fluffing poms wasn't one of them. You might think poms would come out of the box ready to go, but the reality was far from it.

"It's weird — new poms look more like limp mops than cool cheer props," said Sheena Hays, as she inspected a pom in need of fluffing. To fluff, you have to puff and pull each individual strand into style before the pom becomes the fluffy ball we all know and love!

Enter the annual Greenview Middle School cheer squad pom party, a longtime squad tradition. With school back in

YOU'RE INVITED . . . TO THE ANNUAL GMS POM PARTY!

Fluff our poms & have some fun!

Date - September 9

Time - 2:00 p.m.

Place - Brooke Perrino's house: 1298 Coughlan Creek Road

Be sure to bring your swimsuit. When the work is done, we'll hit the pool!

session, we'd chosen this sunny September Sunday to hold the party at my house. And the festivities were in full swing! All twelve members of the team had shown up to whip our new shipment of poms into show-off shape.

It was hard, boring work, but, of course, no party would be complete without a *little* fun. Music, pizza, and hopefully some pool time were all in the plan. Having spent hours designing the invites and helping my mom clean, I was ready to have a little fun myself!

Surveying the scene on the patio, I couldn't help but smile. It felt good to see everyone so excited about a new cheer year. The air crackled with possibility about what lay ahead for us as a squad.

I watched my teammates as they busily pulled shiny blue and red poms from the boxes. There was bubbly, bright Gaby, who seemed to have endless energy. Next to her sat Melissa Marks, or "Lissa" to all of us. A bit of a tomboy, Lissa was a killer gymnast with a heart of gold beneath her tough-acting surface. We could always count on Lissa to speak her mind!

And who could forget Faith Higgins, one of the newest additions to our squad? Shy and sweet, Faith was always willing to lend an ear — or an earring — to anyone in need. Among all of the spirited faces, they couldn't help but stand out. After all, they're my BFFs!

"Snap out of it, B!" chided Lissa with a laugh. "We need you to show us how to do this right. Mine is looking more like a crumply sea creature than a perfect pom."

"Yeah, and mine looks like it came straight out of Bozo the Clown's closet!" joked Gaby, dangling a pom over her head like a wig.

Coach Adkins winked at me as she watched from the doorway. "You show 'em, Perrino!" she yelled. She liked to address us by our last names. I began to demonstrate proper fluffing technique yet *again*.

It was a part I knew well: leader, teacher, role model. Sure, it could be a little stressful sometimes, but I loved helping keep our squad on track. My not-so-secret goal for the year was to be elected team captain, something that both Coach Adkins and the team would have a say in. Usually the honor went to a second-year squad member, and as one of the most involved eighth graders, I thought my chances were pretty good. Not that I'd have to wait long to find out — elections were next week! I was super pumped.

But in the meantime, there were poms to fluff and a party to host. At the sound of the doorbell, I jumped up. Pizza delivery!

"Hey kiddo," said my mom as I surprised her from behind with a hug. "I hope your friends are hungry! We've got pineapple, mushroom, sausage, veggie — pretty much the whole pizza spectrum."

I raised my eyebrows. "Are you kidding me? This is the GMS cheer squad we're talking about! I'm pretty sure most of us have bottomless pits for stomachs."

"Well, hey, all that jumping and yelling burns off lots of calories," said Mom with a knowing smile. "You need nourishment . . . and you deserve a treat every once in a while!"

Truer words had never been spoken. While Mom set up the pizzas on the counter, I called the girls to come grab some slices — in my loudest cheer voice, naturally! Everyone lined up as Faith passed out the paper plates, and soon everyone had heaping piles of pizza.

"This isn't just a meal break, ladies. It's meeting time," called Coach Adkins from the patio. The picture of efficiency, she was never one to waste a spare moment. "Circle up!"

We all went outside and sat down, forming a circle with knees touching, another GMS tradition. Coach Adkins started with some announcements about future practices and games. We also brainstormed some ideas for the big pep rally to kick off the first football game of the year. People started throwing out ideas, some of them more colorful than others.

"How about getting a pop star to record our school song?" asked Gaby. Another teammate, Trina Mathews, suggested passing out Juicy sweatsuits in school colors — something Lissa, our fund-raising chair, quickly shot down.

Then came the part that most perked up *my* ears — the scoop on the captain election. I sat up straighter as Coach A went over how they would work.

GO BANANAS!

At pep rallies, skits and games are good for a laugh. I read about this one in one of my cheer magazines. I would love to do this at a big rally!

* Organize a banana-split-making contest.
  Divide the featured sports team into groups
  of five. Have one person from each group
  lie on the ground, holding a bowl. The other
  teammates take turns standing on a chair
  and dropping banana split ingredients into
  the bowl. The first group to make a split
  wins!

Make sure to have a prize for the winners, and
fresh T-shirts for the bowl holders.

"Applications are due•at practice tomorrow," she explained. "After all of them are reviewed, I'll pick six finalists to interview, after which the field will be narrowed to four girls."

Mackenzie Potz raised her hand. "Do we get a say in picking captain?" she asked. I knew she was interested in applying.

"Yes, the team will vote on the four finalists," Coach Adkins began, but I was barely listening at this point. I was too busy picturing my reign as captain. *Me, leading practices, making up routines, accepting trophies at competition . . .*

Yet before I could get too deep into daydream land, Coach Adkins snapped me out of it with a surprising twist. "Before we finish the meeting, I want to share one thing we'll be doing differently this year," she said, pausing as some squad members threw out teasing "oohs" and "aahs" in suspense. "We're going to have *two* captains. Co-captains!"

Whoa! What? I couldn't believe what I was hearing. Sharing the spotlight — *and* the power. Would this change be twice as nice or double trouble? It was hard to tell. I shook it off and took a deep breath. For now, I just wanted to enjoy an easy, breezy afternoon surrounded by my best buds in the world.

"Last one in the pool has to fluff the rest of the poms!" I yelled, jumping up and getting a running start. Laughing, everyone jumped in the water one by one — fully clothed! Yep, this year was going to be *full* of adventure. And I couldn't wait.

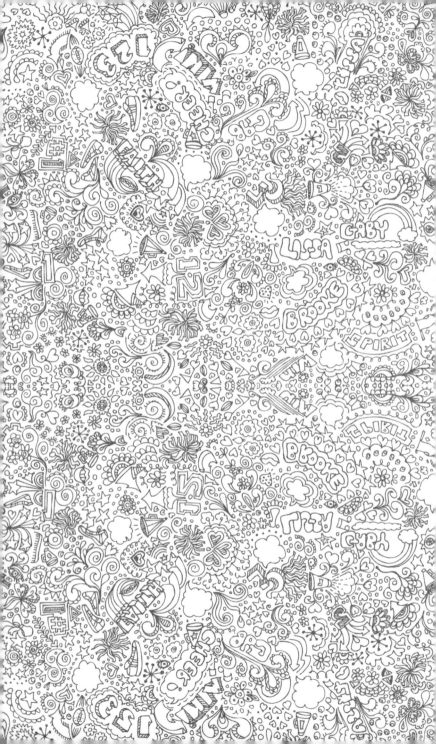

Chapter 2

Some people dread Mondays, but personally, they always put a little pep in my step. C'mon, I'm a *cheerleader*. It doesn't take much! I really love the feeling of diving into a new week. The hustle and bustle of going to classes. The excitement of games, practices, and other cool cheer stuff. I guess I've always loved being busy. Hard work doesn't scare me off!

Of course, I try not to be *that* girl. You know, the one who always has her hand up with the answers? Or the one who does it all — student council, glee club, cheer, you name it. But sometimes I can't help it. It's just how I'm built!

So when Gaby asked me to help her out with English before school started in the fall, I didn't even blink an eye. She'd really struggled through seventh grade, and she wanted to start this year off on the right note.

We decided to meet on Mondays before practice in The Nook — a gathering area our school shared with the high school. It was kind of cool. Not only were there cute high school boys to gawk at, but there was also a healthy snack bar and lots of big beanbags to lounge on. Sometimes they even showed stuff like music videos and Disney flicks after school!

"Ooh, maybe we should forget English and veg out in front of the tube — or just check out the scenery," said Gaby, making eyes at a guy a few feet away. Out of all of my cheer friends, she was definitely the biggest flirt!

I gave her a look, and she conceded that we had a job to do. We found a quiet area and plopped down at a table. "So why exactly do participles dangle again?" said Gaby, giggling. "Is it like when a cheerleader gets all wobbly in a stunt?"

I grinned, but felt a little pang inside. I knew Gaby was kind of ashamed that she struggled in school. She loved to make jokes, but sometimes it was her way of coping. "Who knows why they dangle?" I joked back. "Probably something that Shakespeare and his posse decided, and it stuck."

With only a half hour before practice, we decided to get serious and try to get some work done. It was actually kind of fun showing Gaby sentence structure and diagramming, although it was tough to get her to stop drawing squiggly lines, stars, and smiley faces around the diagrams! But for the most part, I was really happy with the progress we were making.

Near the end of our meeting, Lissa stopped in to say hi. She usually ran home during the break between school and practice to walk her bulldog, Dixon. "Hey guys, what's up?" she huffed, a little out of breath. She grabbed a paper from Gaby's notebook. "Is Brooke helping you become the next **Stephenie Meyer** *?"

~~~~~~

* My parents wouldn't let me read Stephenie Meyer's Twilight books until after seventh grade. Then I read all four in about a week!

"I wish!" said Gaby. "Then maybe I could meet Robert Pattinson, and I would be fabulously rich. We could pay for our squad to go to Worlds, no prob!"

It was a funny thought. **Cheerleading Worlds*** were for squads from major all-star gyms, not school teams. Our squad was competitive, but we probably wouldn't be flocking to Florida with the top dogs any time soon!

"Hey, what is this, anyway?" asked Lissa, looking at the paper more closely.

Gaby's eyes widened and she grabbed the paper, stuffing it back into her notebook. "Oh, that. Nothing much."

My eyes met Lissa's. "Out with it, Gabbers. What's the deal?" I asked.

She sheepishly held the paper up for us to see. It was an application for captain! I couldn't believe it. Responsibility and Gaby just didn't go together. This was the same girl who

---

* Imagine yourself at Disney World in Orlando, Florida, surrounded by the most cheerful and energetic people on the planet. You just might be at Cheerleading Worlds. You have to win a qualifying competition just to compete there. It is truly for the best of the best.

CHEER CAPTAIN APPLICATION

Name: Gaby Fuller

Grade: 8th   GPA: 2.75

List your previous cheer experience, including classes and camps.

I started cheering in 2nd grade, and I've been dancing ever since I can remember. I've been to cheer camp for the last two summers, along with the rest of the GMS team.

What leadership positions have you held?

I haven't really had any leadership positions with a title or anything. But I think that rest of the squad looks to me for leadership with our dances. And I am always there to make everyone laugh when it gets stressful!

What would your main goal be as captain of the squad?

I think it is important that the captain includes everyone and makes them all feel important. I want to help keep the squad's spirits up, even when it gets super busy and stressful. Even though we are cheerleaders, it is nice if someone cheers for us once in a while!

What type of qualities would you look for in a co-captain?

Enthusiasm, a positive personality, and someone who really has it together.

* Parent or guardian information:

I, ___Jane Fuller___, give my child permission to apply for and, if selected, serve as the Greenview Middle School cheer captain.

Guardian's signature: *Jane Fuller*

regularly blew off homework for shopping sessions at the mall. The same girl who was always ten minutes late to everything. The same girl who happened to be one of my *best friends*. And she wanted to run the squad? And run against *me*?!

I felt myself turn red. I wasn't sure what to say. I'd wanted this for so long. And I really needed the support — and votes — of my closest friends!

Gaby sensed my mood shift and tried to break the tension. "Brooke-y, you know I would never run against you if there was just going to be one captain," she said. "But I think this might be really good for me. I need to step things up in my life, and cheer is the one thing I'm confident about."

I felt myself relax a little. She was right. There was a chance we could both get captain. And I really had no right to get all territorial about the job. I forced a tiny smile and put my arm around Gaby.

"Well, we better get to practice so we can turn in our applications to Coach A," I urged. "Or else Ella Jenkins might beat us to it!" We all groaned. Ella really was one of "those girls." She meant well, but she was pretty annoying.

At the thought of bossy Ella being captain, we all stood up at the same time and started laughing uncontrollably. "Let's go!" we said in unison. At least we were on the same page about *that*.

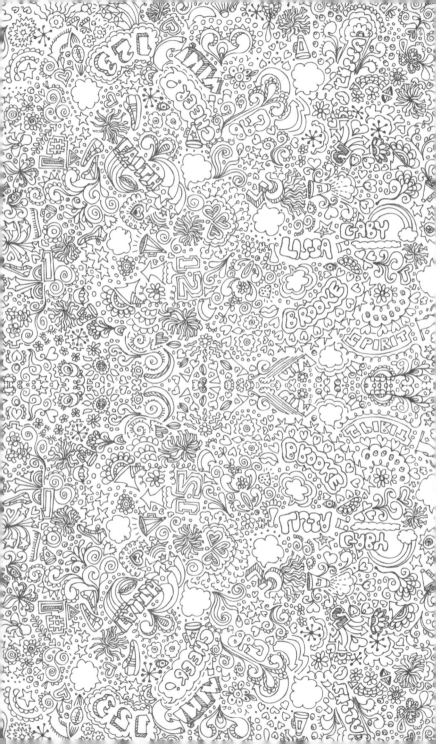

Chapter 3

"Okay, let's run the routine one more time," said Coach Adkins, clapping her hands with authority. "The pep rally is less than two weeks away, and I want it to be perfect!"

"Yeah, this is our first big show of the year, and we really need to shine," echoed Ella. I couldn't help but think she was kissing up to Coach A! But despite myself, I couldn't have agreed more.

"Well, it was definitely a big hit at **cheer camp***," remembered Faith aloud. Some of the other squad members nodded

---

* Every year, our team goes to cheer camp at Rosen College. You can't imagine all the stuff we learn in just three days of camp!

in agreement. We'd spent a lot of time practicing the routine over the summer and had debuted parts of it at camp.

Kicking it off was a high-energy dance and tumbling sequence, followed by a few crowd participation cheers. Not only were there several tricky formation changes, but the routine also featured a group stunt at the end. It was definitely a toughie, but I had faith we could pull it off.

"Music ON!" barked Coach A, after we hit our starting places. "Five, six, seven, eight!"

Notes of Black Eyed Peas filled the air, and Lissa took a running start for her **full-twist tumbling pass***. No easy feat! While the rest of us rocked the choreography, Ella and Kacey crossed the front with **round-offs into back handsprings****.

* Lissa is like a little powerhouse when she launches into her full-twist tumbling pass. A back flip + a 360-degree twist = AWESOME.

** Back-to-back moves, like a round-off to back handspring, really get the crowd going. A round-off starts like a cartwheel but ends with the legs snapping together and feet landing at the same time. That puts the girl in perfect position for the back handspring. The tumbler springs back onto her hands, then over onto her feet.

They landed on either side of the room, where large signs reading "G" and "O" were waiting in place. After the last pose of the dance, they picked up the signs, and we started our chant.

 Gimme a G – G! O – O! Go, Vikes, go!

We yelled the chant several times to the imaginary crowd, hitting the motions with strength and confidence. It's really important to do everything full out, even when you're just practicing! Coach A is a much tougher crowd than two-hundred excited fans anyway.

During the chant, Ella and Kacey took turns holding up the signs as we moved into a new formation. The chant ended with us lifting Ella and Kacey into **chairs***, as they proudly held the signs high.

~~~~~~~

* Let's see...how do I explain a chair stunt? Well, a base holds the flyer high in the air above her head by supporting the flyer's bottom with one hand. Meanwhile, the flyer bends one knee, tucking her foot at the base's elbow. The flyer's other leg remains straight, with the base holding the flyer's ankle for support. The stunt gives the girls more height, and having those "G" and "O" signs a bit higher makes a big impact!

"Yeah! Way to hit it!" yelled Coach A in encouragement, as we promptly led into the cheer.

Cheers with stunts can be really challenging. You, of course, need to yell and get the crowd involved. Meanwhile, you are either in the air or *holding* someone in the air, and the person you're holding probably doesn't weigh much less than you. I challenge anyone who thinks cheerleading is a piece of cake to try on *our* skirts for a day!

I'm a flyer, which means that I get to be on top of the stunts. As a flyer, all eyes are on you. Even when you're scared, you have to paste on a smile and make it look like you're having the time of your life.

Luckily for me, I would trust my stunt group with my life. A stunt group usually has several bases, whose job is to support and hold the flyers up. My stunt group included Faith, Mackenzie, and Sheena. Sometimes we rehearsed together outside of practice, which was good for team-building. When stunting together, trust and friendship are a must!

"Load in for libs!" yelled Coach Adkins as we reached the cheer's halfway mark. At this point, the bases' big job was to raise me to **elevator*** position, after which I would hit a liberty.

For a liberty, one of the flyer's feet is in the bases' hands, while the other leg hits a pose like a **heel stretch** or **scorpion****. It's definitely a balancing act! An easier stunt, the elevators, allowed us to do a level change and make things more visually interesting. Plus, the audience is always more impressed when we yell from the top of a stunt.

"Viking fans, on three, yell 'Blue!'"

I could hear Lissa's voice above the others in front. She, Kate, Maddie, and Britt usually filled the roles of dancers or gymnasts. They rarely did partner stunts. Instead, they got the crowd riled up from the floor during the cheers.

~~~~~~~~

* I love how it feels to be on top of an elevator stunt. I stand with my feet in the hands of my base stunters. The bases hold me at their shoulder level.

** For a heel stretch liberty, I hold my unsupported leg by the foot high to the side, pointing my toes for a finished look. For a scorpion, the leg goes behind me and I hold it with both my hands. Can you say "arched back?"

"1-2-3-BLUE!"

I glanced down to see them shouting through their megaphones and felt energized. Spirit was in the air! I shouted the final words of the chant.

"All together, let's hear you yell, 'blue and red!'"

During the words "blue and red," we reloaded, and I hit my liberty to finish strong.

Suddenly, I heard a thud to my left. Looking over, I saw that Gaby had fallen out of the other stunt. My group quickly cradled me, and we ran over to make sure she was okay.

In typical Gaby fashion, she stood up and rubbed her butt for some comic relief. "Now that was an ending to remember!" she exclaimed. The rest of us let out relieved sighs. "I guess I was a little . . . distracted," she added, avoiding my eyes.

Faith shot me a puzzled stare, and I just looked down. I felt terrible. The whole captain conversation replayed in my head. I hadn't meant to make Gaby nervous. Before I could say anything, Coach Adkins came over to join us. "These things happen," she assured us. "Fuller, you sure you're okay?"

At Gaby's nod, Coach Adkins asked us to sit down so we could go over some performance notes and wrap things up. I only half-listened, thinking about Gaby, the captain applications, and my upcoming algebra test. My mind was swimming! Before I knew it, Coach Adkins was standing over me with her hand outstretched. "Perrino, I'm collecting apps — I believe you have one for me?" she asked sternly.

"Oh, yes! It's right here," I answered, pulling the application out of my backpack. Coach Adkins continued to walk around the circle, collecting papers from Gaby and several others.

I was a jumble of emotions — excited, nervous, impatient, and still feeling kind of bad about Gaby's fall. But most of all, I was filled with anticipation. Being captain was just a piece of paper away!

CHEER CAPTAIN APPLICATION

Name: Brooke Elizabeth Perrino

Grade: 8th   GPA: 4.0

List your previous cheer experience, including classes and camps.
I have six years of cheer experience. I attended several day camps in 4th, 5th, and 6th grades, then the UCA camp at Rosen College the summers before 7th and 8th grade.

What leadership positions have you held?
I was class president in 6th grade, and this year I am on Student Council. I'm the secretary.

What would your main goal be as captain of the squad?
I would keep the squad organized, and make sure everyone is where they are supposed to be and knows what they are supposed to be doing. I would also lend a helping hand whenever needed! I am certain I can lead this team to victory.

What type of qualities would you look for in a co-captain?
Responsibility, creativity, and a positive attitude — qualities I like to think I have myself.

* Parent or guardian information:

I, _____Lilly Perrino_____, give my child permission to apply for and, if selected, serve as the Greenview Middle School cheer captain.

Guardian's signature: *Lilly Perrino*

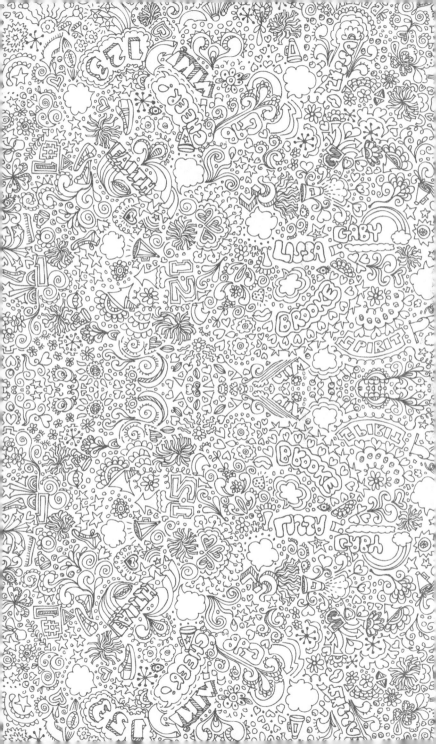

Chapter 4

Ever feel like you're on a treadmill that is set on mega-speed? Welcome to my hectic world. The week flew by, and I felt like I could barely keep up with everything. Eighth-grade honors classes were proving to be way harder than seventh grade. And when I didn't have my nose buried in my own homework, I was usually helping Gaby or someone else with theirs.

On the day of the captain interviews, it was Gaby's turn to help me for a change. Ever the fashionista, she'd offered to come over before school and comb my closet for a suitable interview outfit. And if I didn't have anything suitable? No problem! She had reserves at the ready.

"Just in case, I brought over a few wardrobe staples," Gaby told me, holding up a pale blue cashmere cardigan and sleek black trousers.

"Now I know how all those Hollywood celebs feel. I've got my own personal stylist!" I joked, feeling myself start to relax. So this was what it was like to get off the treadmill for a bit.

INTERVIEW WARDROBE

What am I going to wear?

-Maybe my brown pants with my white sweater and some sort of scarf?

-Or what about my gray skirt with a nice button-down shirt? Too dressy?

 -Jeans and a cardigan? Is that too casual?

"Actually, I don't think you need one, Brookie," said Gaby, looking through my closet. "You've got some really cute stuff in here!" Our styles were definitely worlds apart: she was girly and feminine, while I liked to wear bright colors and bold prints. It was good to get the Gaby seal of approval!

After I modeled several outfits of Gaby's choosing, we'd settled on a chic fitted jacket with matching pants. It was both pretty and professional.

A few short hours later, I was outside Coach A's office, waiting for my turn to interview. Gaby was inside taking her turn. I couldn't help but wonder how it was going.

As soon as I saw her giant smile, I knew it had gone well. "Thanks again, Coach A!" she called, her long floral skirt swishing as she skipped out of the office. She'd probably had her outfit planned for days!

"Good luck, girl," she whispered as we passed.

"Perrino!" Coach Adkins greeted me. She shuffled some papers around on her desk, pulling my application out of the pile. I breathed in sharply, trying to calm my nerves. I knew I was the best person for the job. I just needed to convince Coach A.

"Well, it's clear that you have a true enthusiasm for cheerleading," said Coach Adkins, glancing at my application. "Why does the team mean so much to you, Brooke?"

"Where do I start?" I said, smiling and shaking my head in awe. "Not only have I made the best friends in the world through cheerleading, but it has also taught me so much about myself. I've pushed myself harder than I ever thought I could, and I love being part of such a successful, close-knit squad. I've also discovered how to be both a team player and a leader. Now I'd like to take on an even bigger leadership role as captain."

And if not captain, Miss America! I thought, giggling inside. I sounded like I was in a pageant of some sort with that answer.

"So I see," said Coach, making some notes in the margins. "And why do you want to be captain, Brooke?"

I suddenly drew a complete blank. I'd never really thought about it. Stuff like this was just what I did. I didn't just join committees; I was always the head of them. With my friends, I was rarely a follower, always the leader. It wasn't like I'd had a lightbulb moment and realized I wanted to be captain. I just assumed I would take the role, like always.

I stuttered a little. "Well, um, I really like getting involved in things," I answered. "I like to be at the center of the action and make decisions." Not a terrible answer, but not exactly an Obama-worthy speech, either.

She nodded and made some more notes. Then she threw out a real zinger: "So, besides you, who do you think would make the best captain?"

I was thrown again. Out of loyalty, I probably should have said Gaby. Yet much as I loved her, I didn't feel that she would be a very good leader. Deep down, I felt that Mackenzie would make the best co-captain. I decided to tell the truth.

"I think Mackenzie would be an excellent choice," I said. "She's

WHAT I HOPE COACH A IS WRITING:

-dressed nicely for interview

-loves the squad, ready for bigger leadership role

-has lots of confidence in interview

WHAT SHE MAY ACTUALLY BE WRITING:

-disloyal to her friends

-overconfident

-not a great answer about WHY she wants to be captain

super smart and creative, and I'm sure she could make up some amazing routines. Plus, everyone likes Mackenzie, so she can keep spirits high when things get stressful."

Coach A raised her eyebrows. It was hard to tell what she was thinking. "I'm sure Mackenzie would appreciate the vote of confidence," she said, finally smiling in encouragement. "Brooke, that's all the questions I have. Is there anything else I should know about why you'd be a great captain?"

"I'm totally dedicated to our squad, and I've got lots of Greenview spirit," I said passionately. "There is nothing I would love more than to devote all of my time and energy to making our team the best it can be!"

"Duly noted," said Coach Adkins, glancing at her watch. "It's almost time for Kacey's interview, so that will be all. Thanks, Perrino!"

I thanked her in return, and gathered my things to leave the office. Once outside, I leaned against the wall to compose myself. The interview was finally over! I thought my chances of being one of the final four were pretty darn good. But it was hard to ignore the little pang of guilt about not recommending Gaby as co-captain, especially after her help that morning. I might be a great captain candidate, but I wasn't feeling like a very good friend.

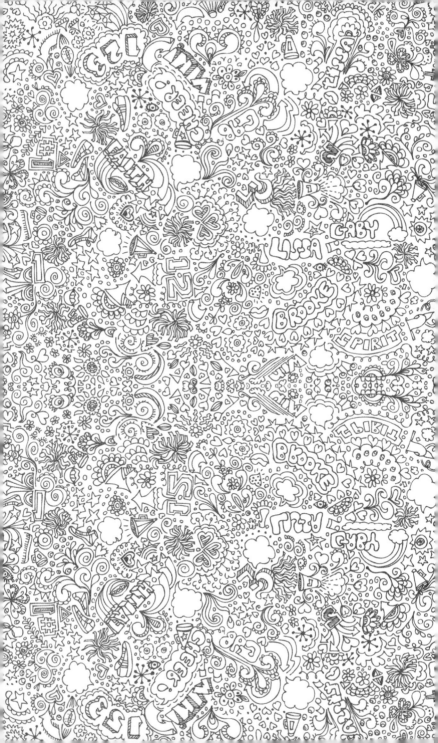

Chapter 5

It had been a long day, but it was far from over! Once I finally got home from school, I knew I'd have to buckle down and do my algebra homework. Studying on a Friday wasn't much fun, but it was necessary. This week I'd really struggled to find time to study, which was a problem considering we had a big test coming up. Now I was tucked away in my bedroom, trying to cram!

If I had to be surrounded by books, at least I was on my bed. It was my favorite place to study. My mom had totally tricked it out with a super-fluffy down comforter, really soft

T-shirt sheets, and lots of colorful throw pillows. Normally, it felt like a fun treat to lounge and get all my studying done in comfy style. I'd throw on my super-study tunes playlist and get to work.

But today the biggest equation on my mind wasn't exactly an algebra problem. It was more like: Brooke + X = co-captains? I couldn't stop thinking about it now that the interview was over.

I tried to refocus and concentrate. Algebra was already tough for me to wrap my head around. Traditionally, I'd always been really good at the right-brain stuff: English, reading, social studies, history. Not so much on the math and science front. Of course, for a self-professed

My super-study tunes playlist, a.k.a. movie scores I love!

1. Lord of the Rings: The Fellowship of the Ring

2. Pride and Prejudice

3. Titanic

4. Harry Potter and the Prisoner of Azkaban

5. Up

6. Ratatouille

7. Life Is Beautiful

8. Forrest Gump

9. Good Will Hunting

10. Beauty and the Beast

nerd like me who usually made straight As, a disappointing grade was usually a B.

But still, I wanted to do well in all of my classes. Pesky polynomials were currently keeping me from doing just that. And worrying about captain elections wasn't exactly helping matters!

Ding! A welcome distraction — my phone vibrated with an incoming text message:

B! You're on my brain. How did your interview go? F.

Faith. She was such a sweetie. She always seemed to just know when I needed to talk. It was hard to imagine a time before Faith was part of our cheer team. She had moved to Greenview a few months ago and joined the squad when another girl moved away. And boy, were we glad she did! We'd all become fast friends, and I loved her positive energy.

I decided to take a break and speed-dialed Faith for a quick chat. Maybe she could help my clear my head and then I could finally focus on algebra.

"Hey, girl," I greeted her. "I *so* need a latte."

"Uh-oh, another marathon study session?" asked Faith. "You're the queen!"

"It's not just that," I confided. "I'm feeling overwhelmed with everything. Classes, cheer, all the usual stuff. And I'm dying to know who Coach A is going to pick."

"Yeah, how did it go?" asked Faith. "I talked to Gaby, and she said her interview went really well."

I narrowed my eyes, trying to ignore my momentary jealousy. I told Faith all about the interview, including the parts where I choked on the "why" question and recommending Mackenzie.

She was quiet for a moment. "Sooo, you didn't say Gaby?" she finally asked. "Mackenzie's cool and all, but . . . well, Gaby's our girl."

"I was just being honest," I said in my own defense. "You know I adore Gabs, but she's not exactly the most reliable person around. It's kind of a requirement that the captain, you know, show up to practices!" I was mostly kidding, but part of me wasn't.

"I hear what you're saying, but Gaby puts her heart and soul into the squad," said Faith gently. "She's got more spirit in her little finger than most people will ever have! This would really mean a lot to her. And I bet you two would have a blast working together."

I felt confused. Maybe I should have given Gaby more of a chance. "It's not up to me, anyway," I said, shrugging it off. "Time will tell!"

I glanced at the clock. "Speaking of time, I should scoot. There's only a half hour until dinner, and I have to finish this algebra homework so I can practice our pep rally routine later."

"All right, good luck with everything," said Faith. "Call me later if you can! In the meantime, I'll be practicing writing your names for the voting ballots next Wednesday. Ha! Bye."

I listened to the phone click and stared at the ceiling. *When did everything get so complicated?* I wondered. For a second, I flashed back to the days when we were little kids cheering for fun on the playground. I almost wished I could travel back in time. All that seemed to matter then was dancing around, being silly, and waving our pom-poms.

It was all about fun. Maybe I needed to lighten up. But first, algebra called: $4x - 2x + 7 = 15 \ldots$

And I got washed away in a sea of numbers yet again.

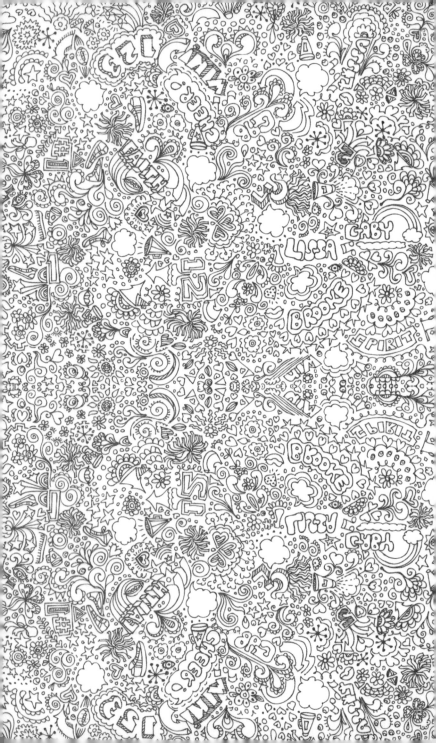

Chapter 6

Almost a whole week had gone by, and captain voting was already behind us. After interviews, Coach A had chosen her four finalists — Gaby, Mackenzie, Ella (eek!) and me! Normally, I would have obsessed about how everyone voted. But with our big pep rally just one day away, I had other things on my mind.

Coach Adkins had asked us to stay after school and make big run-through banners for the rally and the first game of the season. You might wonder: why bother making a sign if a bunch of burly football players are going to bust right through it? A valid question, no doubt. Yet run-through signs are a tradition at Greenview Middle, just like they are at lots of schools. They help the teams really make an entrance and get all pumped up before a game. And as cheerleaders, it's our job to create that spirit — for the team and the crowd. Even if all our pretty artwork gets torn to pieces in a matter of seconds!

"Do we get to stuff the candy bags today, too?" asked Gaby eagerly. Along with making signs, creating little candy bags to put in the players' lockers was something we did before almost every game. Sometimes before really big games, we even decorated the boys' locker room with crepe paper and "Good Luck" signs. But the candy was Gaby's favorite part. She had a serious sweet tooth!

"No, we won't have time for that," said Ella rudely, rolling her eyes. "We have to make hallway signs, plus the run-through banners."

"Point taken," said Gaby, pulling a box of Junior Mints from her cheer duffel. "I love working on run-throughs! We should make it really splashy. Maybe we should draw a huge

OTHER COOL STUFF WE DO ON GAME DAYS:
- -

* One time, we took a bunch of oranges and wrote messages on them. Then we left them in the locker room for the players to snack on.

* For special night-time football games, we hand out glow necklaces. The stands look too cool!

* Sometimes we make the game day a special spirit day. Students are allowed to wear hats and sunglasses for the day. (We get the principal's permission!) It puts people in a good mood for the day.

Viking helmet and have it say 'Hats off to the Vikes!'" Some of the other squad members nodded enthusiastically.

"I don't know. Don't you think it should be more simple?" I asked. "Maybe we could draw G-M-S in huge block letters or something."

"That's kind of boring," said Lissa with an apologetic look. "What if we make one that's focused on victory? It could say 'Beat the Bears' and show a picture of a Viking capturing a bear."

At that, everyone started buzzing and debating ideas among themselves. Our voices bounced off the walls of the gym and seemed to get louder and louder. Coach Adkins shushed us and tried to create order again.

"Girls! We have the whole season ahead of us. I'm sure we'll find a way to use all of these ideas," she said. "Why don't we start with Gaby's idea and use that one for the pep rally?"

Everyone seemed cool with that, so Kate and Mackenzie unrolled a big sheet of paper and taped it down to the floor. Our canvas was ready!

"Kacey, you're a rock star at bubble lettering, so can you work your magic?" I asked. She gamely started writing big words across the top of the paper in blue marker. "Meanwhile, the rest of us can work on the smaller signs."

After a while, we really got on a roll. Soon we had a great looking run-through sign and tons of tiny, cute spirit signs.

"My favorite one says, 'GREENVIEW ROCKS!'" said Sheena, holding up a piece of paper with jagged letters and a guitar she'd drawn.

"Mine says, 'IN IT TO WIN IT!'" responded Kate, showing hers off as well.

Coach Adkins then put us in teams of two to go hang signs in the hallways. She paired me with Gaby, which I normally would have loved. But today I felt a little on the edge.

We hadn't talked too much one-on-one since the interviews. I wondered if she felt as weird as I did about the whole captain thing. Not that we had much control at this point anyway — the squad had voted yesterday at practice, and the decision was out of our hands.

Gaby came over and linked her arm through mine, a stack of signs in her other hand. "You ready, *mamacita**?" she asked. Lissa's mom, who was Latino, had made sure Lissa learned Spanish. And Lissa had passed along lots of Spanish expressions. We all loved to call each other stuff like *señorita*** and mamacita.

"*Sí, mami chula,*" I answered with the Spanish words for "yes, cutie." She bumped my hip with hers in response and did a little salsa wiggle. It was one of Gaby's special talents. She always knew how to lift a mood with the simplest gestures.

We ran upstairs to the third floor to start wallpapering the halls. As we walked past one of the math classrooms, I heard someone call my name. It was Mrs. Stephens, my algebra instructor. "Do you have a second, Brooke?" she asked, poking her head into the hallway.

I glanced at Gaby, who nodded in encouragement. "Sure," I said slowly. I wasn't sure what she wanted. "I'll be right back," I added to Gaby.

---

* When we say mamacita, it's like saying "beautiful girl."
** senorita = young lady, which I'd like to think we all are!

Mrs. Stephens shut the door behind us. "Brooke, I meant to talk to you after class, but you ran off so quickly to your Student Council meeting," she said. "I'd like to discuss your grade on today's pop quiz."

I tensed up. The quiz had totally taken me by surprise. Even though I had planned to put in extra study time yesterday, I'd spent half of my time spacing out and the other half chatting with Faith. As a result, I hadn't been as prepared as usual. Could I have a dreaded . . . B?

Mrs. Stephens held up my paper. "You got a 64 percent on the quiz, Brooke. That's a D-minus," she said with a frown. "I just wanted to see if you'd like some extra help. I'd hate for you to fall behind. Honors algebra moves rather quickly, and it's important to understand the basics."

I was scared, insulted, and bummed all at once. So I'd flubbed one quiz. It wasn't the end of the world. I'd bounce back! My 4.0 depended on it. Yet the phrase "D-minus" kept echoing in my head. I wasn't used to hearing those words.

Then Mrs. Stephens said something even more jarring. "Brooke, I know cheerleading is really important to you,"

Part of the horrible math quiz:

3. Add $(2x^2 + x + 1) + (3x^2 - 5x + 2)$

4. Subtract $(2x - 8) - (5x + 4)$

5. Subtract $(3a - 2b + c) - (4a + 5b + 6c)$

6. Find $(-2x^2 + y^2)\ 4$

she continued. "But it's important to find a balance between schoolwork and your extracurricular activities. Don't forget, all athletes have to maintain at least a C in all of their classes to even stay on the squad."

It wasn't something I'd ever had to think about before. My mind scrambled as I tried to think of my grades so far in algebra. I'd gotten a B on the first quiz, and a C-plus on the second one. And now a D-minus. Warning bells rang in my head. I'd really have to start rocking out the algebra to get a passing grade. The test next week really would be a biggie.

"Thanks, Mrs. Stephens," I said, trying to seem put-together. "I'll be sure to let you know if I feel like I'm falling behind."

Greenview Middle School Athletic Eligibility Policy

1. Students' athletic eligibility runs from grading period to grading period, that is, every nine weeks.

2. Students must maintain a 2.0 grade point average.

3. A student may lose eligibility with two or more U's (unsatisfactory) in behavior on a report card.

4. A student who is suspended from school is ineligible during that time. A second suspension or one five-day suspension makes him/her ineligible for the season.

She nodded. "Great, Brooke. I have faith in you. Let me know if you need anything."

I gathered my stuff and rejoined Gaby out in the hallway.

"What was that all about?" she asked.

"Nothing too much," I answered. I didn't want anyone, especially Gaby, to think I had too much on my plate to be captain. "I think she wants me to take on another tutoring gig." Gaby didn't need to know that I was the one who prob-ably needed to be tutored.

"Well, just as long as I get to keep you as my teacher!" said Gaby with a grin. "You get an A-plus in my book."

It was nice to hear, but I felt worried. Hopefully I'd get an A-plus in Mrs. Stephens's book, too.

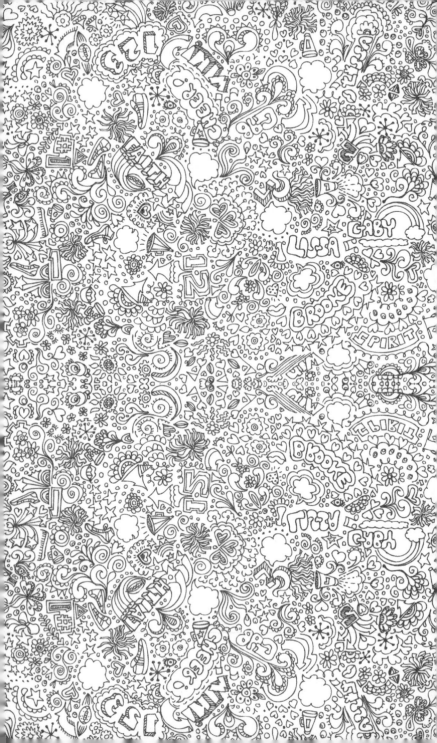

Chapter 7

One of my favorite movie scenes ever is the pep rally part in **Grease***. From the big bonfire to the old-school uniforms, it's just the cutest! For that reason — and many others — I always loved channeling my inner Sandy at our own school rallies.

Of course, ours weren't *quite* as over the top. No bonfires here, but still lots of spirit and fun. I'd been super excited about this rally for ages and was really happy the day had finally arrived. TGIF, indeed!

---

* If I were cast in <u>Grease</u>, the musical from the 1970s starring John Travolta and his dance moves, I'd want to play Sandy. Are you surprised? She's the leading lady!

"It feels like we're really pulling out all the stops for this pep rally," remarked Faith as we walked up the school steps together. Since she was new to cheerleading, she didn't have the experience with rallies and games that the rest of us had.

"This is a *big* season for us," I told her. "You weren't here for football last year, but it was totally crazy! We were the top team in the middle school league up until the last game, and then we lost the championship in overtime by *one* point. This rally has to kick things off right!"

The football players weren't the only ones hungry to take home a trophy. As cheerleaders, our competition season was just starting, too. So as far as we were concerned, this pep rally was just the beginning of a winning year for all!

On a personal note, there was yet *another* reason I could hardly wait for today's rally. Coach Adkins would be announcing the cheer captains to the whole school. I had been going crazy, waiting for the results ever since the squad had finished the process of interviews and voting. Why couldn't Coach A just tell us at a practice or something?

CHEER CAPTAIN VOTING BALLOT

Vote for one

__ Brooke

__ Ella

__ Gaby

__ Mackenzie

I was on pins and needles. Would this be my crowning moment, or would I be watching someone else take the reins?

The school day flew by, and it was tough for me to concentrate. I spent most of last period study hall instant messaging in the computer lab with Lissa instead of working on algebra like I should have. There was just too much to talk about! Which competitions our squad wanted to attend, who would get captain, the new stunts we wanted to try, and, of course, which football players were the cutest. (Definitely Jack Sullivan and Derek Sowers by *far*!)

When I finally decided to buckle down and attack my algebra, another IM popped up. I shot Lissa a sideways look since I'd just told her I needed to study. But it turned out Lissa wasn't the sender. It was from Gaby.

POMPRINCESS98: Hey girl! Just wanted to let you know I got an A-minus on my English essay, and I owe it all to you. You rock my world Michael Jackson-style. I owe you a fro-yo! And just wanted to say good luck on the whole captain thing. I'd be lucky and honored to be your co-pilot. Hearts and xo's!

What a sweetheart, I thought. I couldn't help but feel a little guilty. I had doubted Gaby at pretty much every turn, and she probably knew it. Yet here she was, sending me good luck and thank you notes.

On the other hand, I felt a little annoyed, too. Gaby was suddenly getting great grades, and mine were going down the drain. Totally not her fault, but maybe I needed to start spending less time helping others and more time on my own work.

The IM *ding!* sounded again, earning me a stern glare from the study hall supervisor.

> **POMPRINCESS98:** You there, mamacita?

I quickly muted the volume and typed back.

> **BPBELLA:** Totally here. Just up to my eyeballs in algebra! Congrats on the grade. I'll see you at the rally. Tootles for now.

With a sigh, I closed out of the IM app and clicked back to my homework. I needed to get through this before school was over. But the remaining time seemed to fly by. By the time the bell rang, I'd only gotten through half the problems. (And *that* was a problem!)

Lissa strolled over to my desk. "Finally! That study hall dragged on and on," she complained. "Let's go start getting ready in the locker room! I want to try that cute glitter eye shadow Faith found."

"Why didn't you just wear it to school?" I asked.

"I didn't think our teachers would appreciate the **Lady Gaga*** look so much," said Lissa with a laugh.

———————

* Who doesn't love Lady Gaga? I am dying to do a routine to one of her songs. But we definitely won't wear crazy costumes like hers!

She struck a diva pose and batted her lashes to illustrate the point. I managed a smile, but the butterflies in my stomach were fluttering nonstop. Between my pile of homework and my jittery nerves about getting captain, I felt like a total wreck!

"I'll meet you there," I said. "I have to stop at my locker first."

Lissa shrugged. "Okay, but hurry up! We need our future captain there to get us all pumped up for the big performance."

Her words pepped me up a bit. It was nice to know my friends had faith in me — even if I didn't always believe in myself. The time had come, and all I could do was cross my fingers. With all my heart, I hoped she was right!

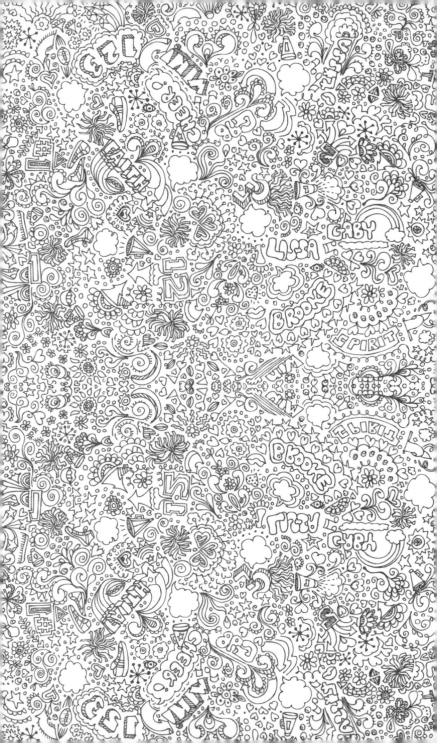

Chapter 8

If you think football teams are the only ones that huddle, think again. One of our prized GMS cheer traditions was the pre-event huddle. No better way to get inspired and excited than to get up close and personal with your teammates! And here we were, head to head yet again with Coach A leading the way. It was almost pep rally time.

"All right, ladies, we've practiced long and hard for this one," she said in her typical gruff voice. "Let's show this school what we've got!" At that, we put our hands into the middle and leaned in a little more. "On three, G-M-S!"

"One, two, three, G-M-S!" we all shouted together, lifting our hands in unison. "G-M-S! Is the Best!"

We all started dancing around and being silly. Faith high-fived me, and we started doing dorky moves like the robot and the lawnmower. The energy was definitely in high gear. We were hiding out in the hallway, waiting to make our entrance for the pep rally.

"Looks like the band is getting ready to start playing," said Gaby, peeking into the gymnasium through the door's window. I got a little chill. I always loved when the pep band played. It was so fun to dance to the fight song and other tunes they played.

Suddenly I heard the sounds of *Stomp, stomp, clap! Stomp, stomp, clap!* coming from inside. The band had started their version of Queen's "We Will Rock You," and the fans were stomping along in the stands. An oldie but goodie, the song always got everyone energized. It was our cue!

We ran into the gym, doing what we called "wildin' out." While making an entrance, we always did lots of jumps, kicks, and tumbling moves. And, of course, spirit fingers.

We got up close to the stands and tried to get the fans on their feet. It was our way of getting the crowd even more pumped up.

After wil-din' out for a few minutes, we took our places for the opening routine. We'd practiced so many times that I felt like I could do it in my sleep. Yet I'd never felt so awake . . . or alive!

♪ **PEP RALLY CLASSICS** ♪
(OLDIES BUT GOODIES)

* "Eye of the Tiger" by Survivor
* "Get Ready for This" by 2 Unlimited
* "Rock and Roll" by Gary Glitter
* "Pump Up the Volume" by M/A/R/R/S
* "The Power" by Snap
* "Unbelievable" by EMF
* "We Will Rock You" by Queen
* "Who Let the Dogs Out" by Baha Men
* "Whoomp (There It Is)" by Tag Team ♫

The familiar Black Eyed Peas song came over the loud-speaker, and the routine began. Except this time we really did have an audience — and they were loving every minute of it.

When I perform in front of a crowd, I always try to remember to . . .

* Be ready. This means have my uniform clean and pressed, pull my hair back, and ditch the jewelry.

* Smile! The crowd won't pay attention if we aren't peppy.

* Keep my head up and make eye contact with people in the crowd.

* If I do make a mistake, I need to just keep going. Panicking won't help, and if I keep that smile on, people might not even notice.

The crowd cheered loudly as Lissa, Ella, and Kacey sprinted across the floor for their tumbling passes. *Wait until they see our stunt at the end,* I thought excitedly.

The chant went off without a hitch, and the crowd yelled along as we held up our signs. Then it was time for the finale — the cheer!

I'd never performed my liberty in front of anyone other than Coach A, but I felt strong and secure. Mackenzie, Sheena, and Faith lifted me into the elevator, and the audience cheered. They were loving it! As we reloaded for the lib, I noticed Gaby's stunt group doing the same out of the corner of my eye. *Whew!* I thought. *No more bobbles.*

We finished the routine with a bang, and I shouted out a "GO VIKES!" before cradling out of the stunt. It felt great to see the crowd so into it. Maybe we could even use this routine for competition down the line. It was really that good!

Coach Adkins approached the microphone. "Let's hear it for the GMS cheer squad," she said, pumping her fist in the air. The crowd played along, hooting and pumping their own fists. "Before we bring in your Viking football team, I'd like to announce this year's cheerleading captains. They'll be leading the squad — and our sports teams — to victory!"

We formed a straight line at center court, grabbing each others' hands. It was time.

Someone yelled from the crowd, "Go Brooke!" In response, people started shouting out other cheerleaders' names in support. It was clear that we each had our own cheerleaders!

I closed my eyes, saying a silent wish. *Say my name, Coach A.*

I didn't have to wait too long. Coach Adkins launched into the announcement. "Your new captains are . . . Gaby Fuller and Brooke Perrino!" she said, turning to smile at both of us. Before I could react, I was getting hugs and pats on the back from every direction. Suddenly our stunt groups lifted us up into shoulder sits in celebration.

From up high, it was just me and Gaby. Our eyes met. "I'm so excited," she mouthed, her eyes wide. And I was, too. We'd both earned this, fair and square.

There wasn't much time to process the info, though. We had a football team to cheer on! The pep band started playing again, this time our school fight song. Gaby and I came down from the stunts and led the rest of the squad in our special fight song dance. We'd be doing this a lot in the coming months.

Near the song's end, we formed two lines that faced each other. With poms in hand, we all raised our arms toward the center. It was time to make a tunnel for the football team to run through!

At the end of the tunnel, Ella and Kacey lifted our run-through sign. The band started up the fight song yet again, and we all started shaking our poms. Coach A handed the microphone to the football coach.

"Everybody on their feet!" yelled Coach Perkins, and we started wildin' out in response. "Are you ready to meet this year's future championship team?"

The crowd started stomping again. All the noise seemed to bounce off the gym walls. "Greenview Middle, here is your Viking football team!" shouted Coach Perkins over the commotion. The boys ran in, busting through our sign and running around the gym floor like maniacs. I jumped up and down, beyond excited.

The votes were in, and Gaby and I were the chosen ones.

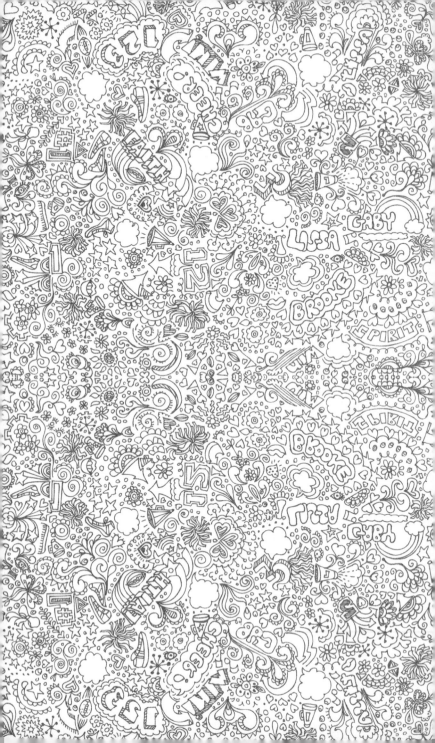

Chapter 9

Whether I would have chosen Gaby as my co-captain wasn't the point, at least not right now. For this moment in time, I was going to soak it in, enjoy myself, and get a little *loco**!

To me, nothing says Friday night like coming home to the overwhelming smell of pasta baking in the oven! I come from an Italian family, and my mom is always cooking up delish stuff like lasagna, ravioli, and homemade pizza. On Fridays, my parents and I have pasta night together. It's our special time to catch up and unwind after a long week.

* loco = Spanish for crazy, as in "Let's get loco and let loose for once!"

I practically skipped into the house, since I was bursting with the good news. I couldn't wait to tell my parents about getting named captain! Mom was in the kitchen, so I ran in and slung my bookbag onto the counter. "Sooooo . . . just call me Captain Brooke!" I squealed, going to give her a hug.

"That's truly fantastic, honey," my mom said, patting my shoulder with her oven mitt. "I'm so proud of you." Was it me, or did her voice sound a little weird? I couldn't put my finger on it. "Why don't you run upstairs and get ready for dinner? You can tell me and Dad all about it once he gets home."

Maybe I was just imagining things. Nothing could bring me down today! I escaped to my bedroom to call Gaby before it was pasta time. She answered her phone on the first ring.

"Hey, superstar," she said with a lilt in her voice. I could tell she was just as jazzed as I was. "I'm at Millions of Milkshakes grabbing a shake to celebrate. I figured, just this once, I could forget about all the sugar!"

"Sure, just this once," I joked. Gaby's sweet tooth had struck again!

"Well, I might as well live it up now. We've got a lot of hard work ahead of us," said Gaby, laughing. "Are we meeting with Coach A next week? I figure she'll want to go over our duties as captain and get the ball rolling."

"I bet she will," I answered. "There is definitely a ton to talk about!"

"Brooke, dinnertime!" I heard my mom yell from downstairs.

"I gotta jet," I told Gab. "Rigatoni calls."

"No prob," she said. "See you tomorrow at the game!"

I bounded down the steps, excited for some pasta and to tell my parents about my day. I was still riding high from the energy of the pep rally! My dad usually got home around dinnertime. He worked as a reporter at our city newspaper, covering environmental issues. I had definitely inherited my love of books and writing from him. I dreamt of following in his footsteps someday.

Dinner was definitely my favorite time with my family. I liked being an only child. It made me feel grown up to talk about current issues and other stuff with my parents. They always treated me like an adult, and trusted me to make my own decisions.

Except . . . when I inevitably messed up every once in a while — like I must have this time. I couldn't help but notice that they both looked really upset as I joined them at the table.

"So, Brooke, I received a call today from Mrs. Stephens," said my dad. My face fell. This couldn't be good. "She's very concerned about your performance in algebra class."

I felt the heat rush to my cheeks. "But —" I started off.

My dad didn't let me finish. "Mrs. Stephens says you've been late with your homework several times, and that she doesn't want to see your grade suffer," he continued. "She also mentioned that you have a big test next week that could make or break your grade."

I sat silent. Sometimes it seemed like nothing I did could please my parents. Lots of people thought I was an over-achiever, but it was just the way I had been raised. Good enough was never actually *good enough*.

"She's right," I said slowly. "I've really been burning the candle at both ends lately, and math sometimes feels like

Greek to me. But let's not forget that I got As on both my social studies *and* English tests this week? I'm not exactly slacking."

"Brooke, we know you're giving everything your all," said my mom gently, serving some pasta onto my plate. "It's just that maybe you're taking on *too* much. Don't you think something has to give?"

"Well, I don't know what that would be," I answered. What were they getting at?

"We think that maybe taking on captain isn't a good idea," said my dad. "It's a huge time commitment, and you already spend half of your time cheerleading as it is. Cheering isn't what's going to get you into Stanford one day."

No way! I couldn't believe my dad was going there. "First of all, people get full-ride college scholarships for cheer leading all the time," I said with a huff. "Secondly, you should be proud of me that I got captain. It's an honor, and being a leader is just as important as being a brainiac."

"We *are* proud, Buggle," said my dad, using his special nickname for me. "We just don't want you to fall behind.

Honors classes move fast, and school comes first."

Hot tears threatened to come spilling out of my eyes. I'd barely been captain for two hours, and my parents were already trying to take it away from me.

My mom sensed how upset I was, and put her hand over mine. "Brooke, we're not going to make any immediate decisions," she said. "But we *would* like you to tone it down until the test on Tuesday. You can cheer tomorrow, but we're asking that you stay in the rest of the weekend to study and relax."

"Fine!" I grumbled, pushing away from the table. "I'll just stay inside doing boring math while everyone else goes out for pizza after the game. Which just happens to be the

A few colleges with cheer scholarships that I've checked out online . . .

* Delta State University
* Fort Hays State University
* Indiana Wesleyan University
* MidAmerica Nazarene University
* University of Delaware
* University of Hawaii (yes, please!)
* Southwest Mississippi Community College

first and most fun game of the season. Have my dinner. I'm not hungry anymore."

I stomped to my bedroom, slamming the door for extra effect. I knew I was being a brat, but I was pretty peeved. And if they were going to treat me like a child, I would act like one!

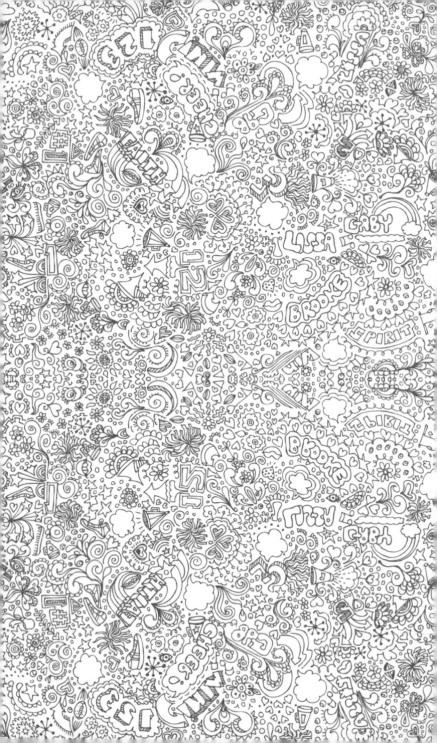

Chapter 10

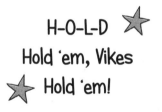

H-O-L-D
Hold 'em, Vikes
Hold 'em!

We were two quarters into Saturday's football game. The other team had the ball, so we were doing some of our new defense chants. Though I was thrilled to be in the thick of things, part of me felt like I was just going through the motions — literally!

It had been another exhausting week, both mentally and emotionally. Plus, I couldn't stop thinking about what went down with my parents the night before. I'd spent most of today sulking in my room, and my parents and I had barely talked on the car ride to the game.

> DEFENSE CHANTS!
>
> Defense, Defense, (clap) Big D
>
> ***
>
> Defense attack (clap, clap)
>
> Push 'em back
>
> ***
>
> Attack (pause) Attack
>
> Defense, push 'em back

I'd insisted they didn't have to come, but there they were, supporting me in the stands. I knew they only wanted what was best for me, but that didn't make it any easier.

I felt a sharp nudge in the side. "Brooke!" Gaby whispered. "You're supposed to call the next chant."

As captains, Gaby and I were supposed to take turns calling the sideline chants. *Get with it, girl!* I told myself. It was time to shake it off and get into the game. I put my hands on my hips and pasted on my best bright smile. "READY?" I yelled to launch us into the next chant. "SET!" the team yelled back.

Take it away
De-fense
Go Big D!

We went through the chant a few times, and then . . . interception! Our team gained control of the ball again. We quickly switched gears and started up a crowd participation chant. As cheerleaders, it was important to keep up with what was happening on the field. There's nothing worse than accidentally doing an offense cheer when on defense, and vice versa! Since we faced the fans, we often had to rely on their reactions to stay on top of things.

Our coach called a time-out to go over some plays. That meant it was time for our squad to take center stage! The marching band started the fight song, and we launched into our trademark choreography — always a crowd favorite.

At the games we always ended the fight song with the same cheer:

WHEN WE SAY, "GO,"
YOU SAY, "FIGHT"
GO, FIGHT! GO, FIGHT!
WHEN WE SAY, "WIN,"
YOU SAY, "TONIGHT!"
WIN, TONIGHT! WIN, TONIGHT!
WHEN WE SAY, "VIKINGS,"
YOU SAY, "ROCK!"
VIKINGS ROCK! VIKINGS ROCK!
GO, FIGHT, WIN, TONIGHT, VIKINGS ROCK
ALL RIGHT, ALL RIGHT!

The cheer ended with the flyers up in **shoulder stands***, shaking their poms and yelling with all their might.

---

* Not sure what a shoulder stand looks like? Well . . . think of the name of the stunt and you should be able to guess. How does the flyer get up there? The base puts her hands behind her back to make a little step, and we climb up.

88

Mackenzie was my stunt partner, so I stood in front of her in the sideline formation.

"It's so cool that we're finally doing the cheers and chants we practiced all summer!" she whispered from behind me. I gave her an excited grin and nodded my agreement. We weren't really supposed to talk on the sidelines, other than to give instructions.

The referee blew the whistle, and the players ran back out onto the field. This game was close. The other team was up 7 to 3, so this was our chance to get ahead!

"Let's do an offense chant to get the energy flowing," I suggested. Whatever we did seemed to work, because before we knew it, touchdown! The crowd went crazy, and so did we —

OFFENSE CHANTS!

Come on, Vikes
Raise that score
Touchdown, touchdown
Six more!

***

Down, down, down the field,
Raise, raise, raise the score,
Down the field,
Raise the score,
Six points more!

doing flips, kicks, and toe touches. "All right, Vikes!" I screamed.

"Drop and give me six!" called Gaby with the drop signal. This year, we were starting a new tradition of doing push-ups every time the team scored. This was our first time to try it.

"One, two, three, four, five, six!" the crowd counted, cheering us on as we did our group pushups. It felt like boot camp, but way better.

At the half, the score was 10 to 7, and it was time for our big halftime show. The game was on our home turf, so we let the other cheer squad take the field first to entertain their fans.

Trina and Ella started giggling and gossiping, but I quickly nipped that in the bud. "Quiet, and hands on hips!" I reminded everyone, ignoring Ella's scowl.

Part of good sportsmanship meant no talking and paying attention while the other team performed. After their show, we clapped politely and yelled things like, "Awesome!" and "Way to go!"

Coach Adkins wouldn't have it any other way. No **Bring It On** * antics on her watch!

And then it was our turn. We ran out onto the field to roaring applause. It was so great to have a supportive fan base! Our plan was to perform the same routine from the pep rally. Only students had seen it so far.

The first note of the Black Eyed Peas song blasted over the loudspeakers, and all of my teammates took action. But what did I do? I just stood there frozen! I couldn't remember the opening dance routine for the life of me. How was this possible?

You've only done this about five zillion times — not to mention that you just performed this yesterday, I told myself in a panic. *Pull it together, Perrino!*

Frantic, I looked at Trina dancing next to me, trying to copy what she was doing. I needed to regain my composure quick! The last thing I wanted was to be the space case that

---

* Bring It On is only my favorite movie ever. My besties and I must have watched this together about 83 times. Nothing beats a cheer competition where two squads have something to prove and you're rooting for both!

doesn't know the routine. I managed to bounce back by the last few eight-counts, but my confidence was totally shaken. I felt so lame!

Afterward, we all met in the girls' locker room to refresh and regroup. I sat in the corner, willing myself not to cry. Some leader I was! I couldn't even get through our first half-time performance without messing up.

Gaby walked over, and I started fiddling with my pom strands. "Hey *chica**, it's no biggie," she said, trying to make me feel better. "It happens to the best of us."

I didn't say anything. I just kept playing with my pom silently, pretending it was the most interesting thing on the planet.

She cleared her throat. "We need to run the halftime meeting. Coach A wants us to go over the sideline dance for between quarters."

"You can do it," I muttered. "I'm not really in the mood."

"I need your help, Brooke," said Gaby. "That's part of what being captain is about. This isn't just about you any-

* chica = girl or girlfriend, as in, "Chica, don't worry about it. You are among friends."

92

more. We need to think about what's best for the team, and pouting by yourself isn't going to cut it."

Wow! Attitude from Little Miss Sunshine. I didn't know whether I was impressed or annoyed. "Okay, okay," I said, standing to join her.

I wasn't trying to be a drama queen, but lately I just felt really alone and overwhelmed. Everyone seemed to be coming down on me! Were my parents right? Maybe being captain just wasn't in the cards. 'Cause suddenly I felt more like a court jester than a queen.

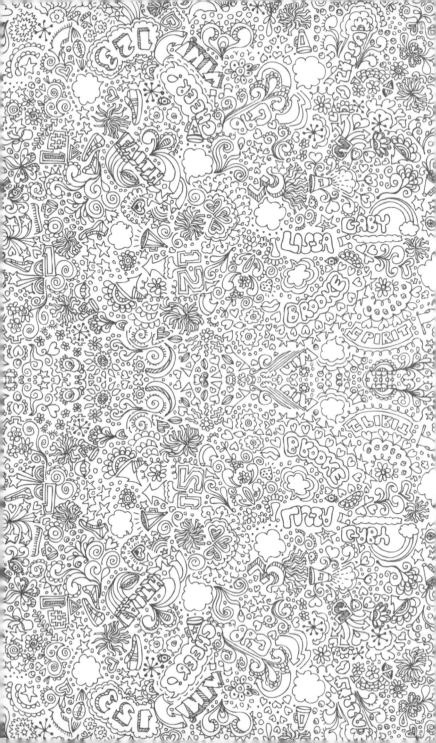

Chapter 11

Back at school on Monday, I felt like I was in a major funk.
The game had definitely been a bit of a downer, even though
we did win. And though I'd spent most of the weekend
studying, I still felt a little lost on my algebra work. Plus, I
hadn't talked to any of my friends since the game. Usually my
phone rang off the hook on Sundays, but I hadn't heard from
Gaby, Faith, *or* Lissa.

After school, I was supposed to meet Gaby for our
weekly tutoring session. I was a little embarrassed about
how I'd acted on Saturday, but I was hoping we could get

SOME OF MY FAVORITE BOOKS

- The Chronicles of Narnia series, by C.S. Lewis

- Freak the Mighty, by Rodman Philbrick

- The Harry Potter series, by J.K. Rowling

- Little Women, by Louisa May Alcott

- The Princess Diaries, by Meg Cabot

- Stargirl, by Jerry Spinelli

- A Wrinkle in Time, by Madeleine L'Engle

back to normal pretty quickly. When the time came, I stopped by my locker to pick up my copy of *A Wrinkle in Time** and headed over to The Nook. It was one of my fave books, and I was excited to escape to another world for a little bit — and show Gaby what it was all about.

Except I never got the chance. Gaby didn't show up! I waited until 3:30, long after our scheduled start time. There were tons of other kids laughing and hanging out, but no sign of Gabs. I tried to read the book to pass time, but I found myself just watching the clock. I probably should have used

* It's no wonder that A Wrinkle in Time has won a bunch of important awards. I love this adventure story. You sort of feel like you are traveling through time and space along with the characters in the book.

the time to study for the algebra test. Now I was *really* in a mood.

I rode my bike home, trying to take in the fresh air and calm down a little. Once I got inside, my mom was nowhere to be found. Usually she was catching one of her soaps or doing some sort of crazy cleaning job. (My mom is a total neat freak!)

"Mom?" I called.

Her voice came from the backyard. "Out on the patio, honey!"

I wandered through the house to go say hello. Upon opening the screen door, I got a major surprise! Around the patio table stood Lissa, Gaby, and Faith next to my mom. On the table were a giant sub, a big bowl of pretzels, and a six-pack of soda, along with math textbooks and some flashcards.

"So, Perrino, we thought you might need some group brainpower to get ready for your big test tomorrow," said Lissa, cracking her gum with authority. "We brought over a survival kit to get you through the night."

My mom smiled. "I figured I could make one exception to the 'no social plans for now' rule," she said.

"Yep!" said Gaby. "By the time we're done here, Einstein and his "e equals mc squared" business will seem like child's play."

For once, I was speechless. "But, Gabs, I thought maybe you were mad at me," I said. "I waited for you . . ."

"Oh, I'm sorry," she said. "I figured you'd want to do your own studying. We all know how important this test is to you! Plus, we were hoping to surprise you. No matter what, we've always got your back."

A wave of gratitude washed over me. They really were always there for me — even despite my diva moments. Feisty Lissa, sweet Faith, and loyal Gaby. A girl really couldn't ask for better friends.

I felt foolish for having ever doubted Gaby. When it came right down to it, she'd really stepped up on Saturday. If I'd been the only captain, our squad probably would have been a disaster!

Suddenly I felt like I — no, *we* — could take on the world. I realized how lucky I was to be co-captains with one of my best friends. How could I have not seen that we would make a great team? Creative, spirited Gaby would be a whiz at choreographing routines, and I could use my organizational and leadership skills to make sure we stayed on track. Together we could be unstoppable!

As for that algebra test? Well, let's just say I didn't ace it, but my grade was good enough to keep me in my parents' good graces for at least a little longer. Making the grade wasn't easy, and I knew being captain wouldn't always be a breeze either. But no matter what, I knew always I'd get by — with a little help from my cheer friends.

The End

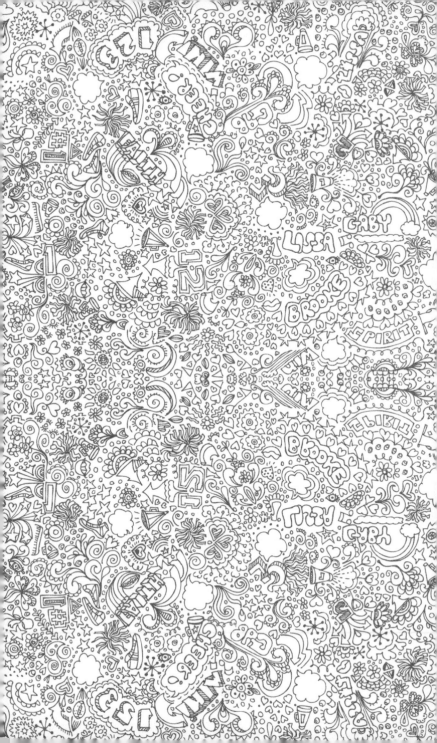

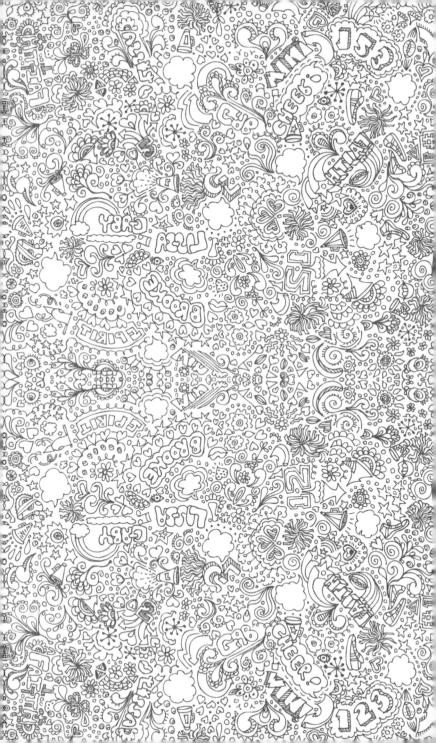

Tell me the truth . . .

So I might have made some mistakes in my quest for captain. Or maybe I didn't! What do you think?

- Do you think I should have stood behind Gaby when Coach A asked who my pick for co-captain was? What would you have done?

- How could I have avoided that whole mess with my algebra grade?

- Do you think my parents were reasonable when they limited my activities to give me study time? What would you have done?

- In your opinion, do I have the qualities needed to be a good cheer captain? Why or why not?

I love to visit the online forums of my favorite cheer magazines. Help me write answers to these questions.

Squad Drama!!!
posted four hours ago by SuperCheerGirl

The girls on my squad cannot get it together. There are two feuding groups, and I am friends with both sides. I feel stuck in the middle. How can I get them to make up already?

Help with my tryout!
posted 1 day ago by CheerNewbie

I'm going to be trying out for cheerleading for the first time ever next week. Any tips for me? How can I deal with my nerves?

Can't find my CENTER!
posted last week by lostleader

I have so much going on with school, cheerleading, my friends, etc. I feel super overwhelmed most of the time. What can I do?

Which cheerleader are you?

Quiz: Are you Brooke, Faith, Gaby, or Lissa? Take this fun quiz to find out which cheerleader you are most like.

1. You forget your homework. You:

A. Make sure to talk to the teacher about it privately. You don't want to draw attention to yourself in class.

B. Turn it in the next day and ask for an opportunity for extra credit so you can make up missed points.

C. Head to the library to tackle it . . . again. Looks like you have to redo it in order to get it in on time.

D. Don't realize it until it's time to hand it in, so you make a joke, give a grin, and promise the teacher you'll turn it in tomorrow.

2. The school play is coming up. You:

A. Volunteer to be a stagehand. You like being involved, but you aren't going to get up in front of anyone.

B. Have no plans to try out. You like to stick to physical extracurriculars.

C. Would love to try out, but will it fit into your busy schedule?

D. Plan to try out. After all, you love to meet new people!

3. You have a free afternoon. You:

A. Paint in your room. You like to spend time by yourself to rejuvenate.

B. Head out for a hike. It will be good exercise.

C. Start with some study time, go on a bike ride, then finalize plans for the party you are hosting.

D. Work on some new choreography. There are some new dance steps you have been dying to add to the school song routine.

4. Cheerleading tryouts are next week. How do you feel?

A. Uncertain. Cheerleading sounds fun, but the limelight is a little too hot for you.

B. You can't wait. You are going to nail that new tumbling pass.

C. Awesome! After tryouts, you will be one step closer to becoming captain.

D. Pretty excited . . . you'll be back with your girls, and making new friends, too.

Quiz continues on the next page!

5. Your favorite thing about cheerleading:

A. Learning a new skill. You had no idea you had it in you.

B. Working toward a common goal, like new uniforms or fees.

C. Helping others learn the cheers and dances so they can do their best.

D. Making posters and goody bags for the teams. It is fun to chat and hang out as we're working.

6. What role do you fill on the squad?

A. New girl — I'm still figuring it out.

B. Treasurer — I can tell you how much money we have (or need).

C. Leader — I like to make sure everyone is in the know.

D. Social butterfly — I see to it that cheerleading is fun for everyone!

7. My family . . .

A. Has a lot of fun coming up with crazy things to do together.

B. Is small, but tight. I can count on my mom for anything.

C. Is proud of me. They encourage me to work hard and be my best.

D. Is loud and fun! It's bound to be, with all those siblings around.

8. When I am with my friends, you can be sure I:

A. Will be a good listener. And if the moment arises, I'll get a laugh or two.

B. Will tell people exactly what's on my mind. I'm sassy like that.

C. Have organized an activity for us. I like making sure everyone is having fun!

D. Will be happy and carefree. And if someone has a fashion crisis, I'll be solving it.

~~~~~~

If you chose:

----> Mostly A — You are Faith. You may be shy, but when you're with your friends or family, you shine with your sweetness and fun sense of humor.

----> Mostly B — You are Lissa. You work hard to meet your goals. Best of all, your friends know they can count on you to be honest and supportive.

----> Mostly C — You are Brooke. You like to be in charge, and you're good at it. If a friend or teammate comes to you, she knows that you will be happy to help her.

----> Mostly D — You are Gaby. You make friends easily and can be counted on to ease the mood. Friends appreciate your spunky style and sheer silliness.

A note from Brooke:

As co-captain, I am supposed to make sure everyone on the squad is upbeat, healthy, and happy. So I'm all about the bonding and much-needed breaks. After all, I don't want any burnt-out cheerleaders on my hands.

I found some great ideas for fun get-togethers that I can't wait to try out on the squad. They were in a book called <u>Cheer Squad: Building Spirit and Getting Along</u>. Check them out:

Beauty Parlor Party

Set up stations like they have in beauty parlors. Make one station for painting your nails, another for doing your hair, and one more for putting on makeup. You'll feel more relaxed and more beautiful by the end of the party.

Movie Marathon

Snuggle into your pajamas for a night of classic cheer and dance movies. Some perfect picks are *Bring It On!* and *Center Stage*.

Spread the Cheer

Go to a game for a sport that your squad doesn't normally cheer for, and make some noise in the stands. The team will be tickled, and you'll have a blast showing your support for them.

Cheer-O-Ling

During the holidays, put a twist on the traditional caroling. Entertain your neighbors with holiday songs-turned-cheers. (Make sure to bring a grown-up with you for safety reasons.)

Fun ideas like these can really put the cheer back in cheerleading!

* Excerpt from *Cheer Squad: Building Spirit and Getting Along* by Jen Jones, published by Capstone Press, 2006

Meet the Author:
Jen Jones

Author Jen Jones brings a true love of cheerleading to her Team Cheer series. Here's what she has to say about the series, cheerleading, and reading.

Q. What is your own cheer experience?

A. I absolutely love cheerleading! I cheered from fifth grade until senior year of high school, and went on to cheer for a semi-pro football team in Chicago for several years. I've also coached numerous teams, and I write for a few cheerleading magazines.

Q. Did any of your family members cheer?

A. Some families are into football — mine is into cheerleading! My mom was a coach for close to 20 years, and my sister cheered throughout grade school and high school. My aunt and cousins were also cheerleaders.

Q. Which cheerleader from the series are you most like?

A. I would say I am probably a combination of Gaby and Brooke: Gaby for her outgoing, bubbly nature, and Brooke for her overachieving, go-getter side. In certain situations, I wish I could channel some of Lissa's feisty fabulousness!

Q. What sort of goals did you have when writing the series?

A. My goals were to create relatable characters that girls couldn't help but like, and also give readers a realistic look at what life on a young competitive cheer squad is like. I want readers to finish the book wanting to be a member of the Greenview Girls!

Q. What kind of reader were you as a kid?

A. I loved to read and often brought home dozens of books every time I went to the library. Whether at the dinner table or in bed, my nose was ALWAYS in a book. Some of my favorite authors were Judy Blume, Lois Duncan, Lois Lowry, Paula Danziger, and Christopher Pike.

Read all of the Team Cheer books

#1-Faith and the Camp Snob

#3-Lissa and the Fund-Raising Funk

#4-The Competition for Gaby

TEAM CHEER!

The best thing about middle school!

FIND OUT MORE ABOUT OUR TEAM

Plus, download fun stuff for you and your friends!